This book belongs to

_____

BRODERICK

by Edward Ormondroyd illustrated by John Larrecq

PARNASSUS PRESS   OAKLAND, CALIFORNIA
HOUGHTON MIFFLIN COMPANY   BOSTON

Evan said,
"You could write a story about that."
So I did, and it's for him.

ISBN 0-590-75949-3

In the broom closet of a
house by a lake there once lived
a young mouse named Broderick.
He was passionately fond of
books. Fortunately for him, the
children of the house loved
books, too. They brought
armloads of them from
the library every week.

The children read the books during the day, and Broderick chewed on the bindings during the night. He always judged a book by its cover.

One night Broderick came upon a book that had been left open. There was a portrait of a mouse on the title page. He was so fascinated that he read the book five times in a row, and forgot to chew the cover.

"Amazing!" he thought. "Why didn't I know about this before?"

He became so eager to read that he couldn't think of anything else. He never chewed on a book now unless it was about cats.

What he particularly loved were stories about famous mice. He simply could not read too often about:

Norman, who was doorman at an art museum, and winner of a sculpture contest; *Amos,* who guided Ben Franklin in almost every important step of his career; *Miss Bianca, Nils* and *Bernard,* who rescued a Norwegian poet from the dungeon of the Black Castle; *Anatole,* who became First Vice-President in Charge of Cheese-Tasting at the Duval Cheese Factory in Paris.*

*Books about these mice are listed in the bibliography in back.

Broderick began to take long walks by the lake, listening to the waves and dreaming dreams of glory.

"I, too, will make my mark in the world," he thought.

The other mice in the house laughed at his ideas. "Just being a mouse is a full-time career in itself," they said. "What more do you want?"

"I want to do something that no mouse has ever done before," Broderick answered. But he didn't know what that might be.

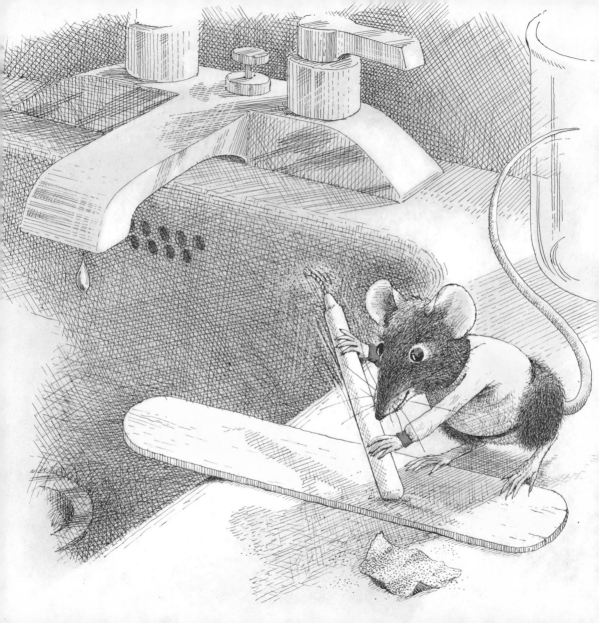

One night there was a different kind of book on the floor. As Broderick read it his whiskers twitched and his tail began to tremble.

"Eureka!" he thought. "Here is my career at last!"

He read the book and studied the pictures for many hours. There was only one thing he needed. In the light of early dawn he searched the house for it from basement to attic. Finally he found an old tongue depressor in the medicine cabinet. Since there was nothing better, it would have to do. He made it smooth with a scrap of sandpaper and waxed it with a candle end.

Then he raced down to the lake, carrying the tongue depressor over his head and shouting, "Surf's up!"

Three minutes later he had his first wipe-out.

Broderick persisted in spite of hundreds of wipe-outs, fatigue, head colds, and other discouragements. In order to be close to his work he built a small cabana on the beach. He spent almost every daylight hour in the water, and many moonlight ones as well. And as the weeks and months went by he gradually mastered the art of surfing.

He learned
to ride the waves kneeling,
then standing.

He learned the pullout, the stall,
the cutback.

He could do
the foot-to-the-rear turn,
the leaning turn, and the
kick turn.

He learned to walk the board,
to ride on one foot,

to do the head dip,

and to hang ten.

As a matter of fact, by using the tip of his tail
he could hang eleven.

By the time he could ride a wave while doing the handstand, Broderick felt that he was ready to make his name in the world. He packed a few simple belongings and said goodbye to the other mice. They all shook their heads, more convinced than ever that he was crazy. It was generally thought that he would come to a bad end.

Broderick smuggled himself aboard an east-bound bus, and had an uneventful trip to the coast. The passengers were so careless with their crumbs that he became

a trifle plump, and had to go on a diet.

One sparkling afternoon the bus arrived at the seaside, and Broderick hopped off. The air smelled deliciously of salt and hotdogs and suntan lotion. Gulls creaked in the sky, and the rumble of surf sounded over the dunes. Broderick's tail began to tremble with excitement. Holding his surfboard over his head, he raced up the warm slope of the dunes.

He never reached the top. Suddenly the sunlight was blotted out, a terrible rustling noise was heard just overhead—and before he could even twitch a whisker he was snatched up into the air by a hungry seagull.

The only thing that saved Broderick from being instantly swallowed was his surfboard, which became stuck crosswise in the gull's bill.

The intrepid mouse quickly recovered his wits. He lashed out with his tail, and in a voice that shook with indignation cried, "Unbeak me, villain!"

The gull was so astonished at the way his lunch was behaving that he dropped it—and Broderick plunged down into the Atlantic.

He kept diving under the surface until the gull became discouraged and flew away. Then he climbed out and sat on his board. The salt water made him blink and sneeze. Something tickled his tail. He looked down and saw a large fish sniffing at it. He jerked it out of the water and wrapped it around his neck.

He had never dreamed that any waves anywhere could be so enormous.

"My doom is sealed," he thought in despair. "If the gulls don't get me, the fishes or one of these waves will. Farewell, fame!"

A huge swell rose under him. As he went up the face of it his surfboard began to slide forward.

"Very well," Broderick thought. "Doomed I may be, but at least I can go to my doom in style."

He stood up, made a smart kick turn to the right, and began to shoot across the face of the wave. He had never gone so gloriously fast in his life. His ears rippled and snapped behind him like flags in a gale. He shouted defiance and shook his fist at fate.

The wave crested behind him. Glancing back, he saw to his amazement that a young man was racing down toward him on a sleek fiberglass board. "Hold your breath, friend!" the young man shouted. He knelt and seized Broderick in his cupped hands just before the collapsing wave wiped them both out.

The young man's name was Tim. He carefully squeezed the water out of Broderick, gave him artificial respiration, and took him home. While Broderick was recovering, Tim made him a beautiful surfboard of balsa wood, and painted it brilliant red.

They decided that Tim would be Broderick's manager, and that they would go on tour together. After a few weeks spent in polishing their routines, they flew to southern California.

Broderick made his professional debut at Malibu Beach. He dazzled the crowd with his sun-bleached fur, deeply tanned tail, and a superb display of hot-dogging.

Wherever Broderick went he created a sensation. Police had to control the crowds. The sale of binoculars and telescopes soared.

When the surf was rough, Tim rode the waves with
Broderick daringly balanced on his finger.

When the waves were small and smooth, Broderick

and Tim surfed side by side with the grace and precision of ballet dancers. Sometimes Broderick rode his board in the bow wave of Tim's board.

On very calm days Broderick took to water skis. He was towed by a battery-powered model boat. When he was going fast enough, a kite fastened to his shoulders carried him high into the air.

He demonstrated his steely nerves by shooting between the pilings of the Huntington Beach Pier.

Broderick and Tim went on a round-the-world tour. Hundreds of thousands of fans watched them surf in Mexico, Hawaii, Australia and Africa. Millions followed every move on television. A documentary film was made of the tour and it became a smash hit.

*   *   *

Wealthy and loaded with honors, Broderick eventually retired from public life. He built a modest chalet on the shore of the lake where he had first learned his art. Here he spent his declining years entertaining, writing his memoirs, and talking to aspiring young mice who flocked from far and wide to hear his words of encouragement.

He also sent a large, anonymous donation to the library. It had always bothered his conscience that he had chewed up so many bindings in his heedless youth.

BIBLIOGRAPHY

Here are some books about eminent mice whose lives and adventures inspired Broderick. They may inspire you, too.

Freeman, Don. *Norman the doorman*. Illustrated by the author. Viking, 1959

Lawson, Robert. *Ben and me*. Illustrated by the author. Little, Brown, 1939

Sharp, Margery. *The rescuers*. Illustrated by Garth Williams. Little, Brown, 1959

Titus, Eve. *Anatole*. Illustrated by Paul Galdone. Whittlesey House, 1956